The Best Holiday Ever!

by

Pete Johnson

First published in 2005 in Great Britain by
Barrington Stoke Ltd, Sandeman House, Trunk's Close,
55 High Street, Edinburgh EH1 1SR
www.barringtonstoke.co.uk

ISBN 1-842993-28-3

Printed in Great Britain by Bell & Bain Ltd

A Note from the Author

There are some holidays you never forget. And a very special one is your first ever holiday without your parents.

Freedom at last! No more parents telling you what to do. No more rows. It's all going to be so brilliant. Yet, things don't turn out quite as you expect. For instance, I never expected that two of my mates would have a row that lasted four days!

When I interviewed some girls they had even more dramatic stories to tell me. Some of which have found their way into *The Best Holiday Ever!*

Of course I also wanted to capture the fun and excitement and drama of such a special holiday. So I hope that's all here too.

But can it really be the best holiday ever?

Well, read on and see ...

Contents

Chapter 1
Hitting Spain

Friday 16th July

It's going to be totally COOL. Two weeks in Spain without any wrinklies. Our first proper holiday. On our own. We can do the things we want to do without getting nagged at all the time.

It's just me (Louise), my best pal Katie and ... well, our mate, the third girl was going to be Sarah. But four days ago she broke her arm. Talk about selfish.

Could we find anyone to go instead of Sarah? We asked everyone we knew. No good, until at last we found out about Annette. She doesn't go to my school and I hardly know her. She lives next door to Sarah's auntie. I'm sure she'll be great.

Saturday 17th July

6.00 p.m. IN SPAIN

We've just reached our holiday flat. It took all day to get here. Yesterday morning, leaving London, seems like years ago. The flat's in an ugly new block. Inside is an even uglier caretaker. He's the guy that looks after all the flats. He's got a bright red nose and a thick beard. ("*He* likes his wine – and lots of it. We can call him Rudolph!" murmurs Katie.) He looks hard at us and frowns.

"Does he know how to smile?" whispers Katie.

He hands us a list of rules. "You must stick to all these rules," he says, "or you will be out of here."

"Thank you for such a lovely welcome," Katie says with a wicked grin.

The three of us walk slowly up the staircase. It's a long way up to our flat and the staircase is dark and a bit smelly.

The best word to describe the flat is "tiny". There's a tiny kitchen, a tiny bathroom and a bedroom. There are two single beds and a sofa-bed with a red and green cover.

"This is mine," cries Annette. She sits down quickly on one of the beds.

Katie whispers, "So who's going to have that funny sofa-bed?"

"I will," I say at once.

I hate it when people make a fuss about things that don't matter.

There's a fantastic balcony. You slide open a huge glass window and there it is! You can almost see the sea. At once Katie and I start pretending to be supermodels. We stretch out across the balcony and lie across the sunbeds. Annette goes into the kitchen and makes some tea. Her mum made her bring some tea bags with her, for godssake!

Katie spots two boys on the balcony below us. They're fast asleep. Katie grins. She runs into the kitchen, gets the wet tea bags and throws them at one of the boys – the one she fancies. A tea bag lands right on his mouth.

He splutters and jumps up. Then he sees Katie and blushes and grins. He shouts up to us that his name is Scott and his mate (still asleep) is Kevin.

Scott's got a black eye.

"How did you get that?" Katie wants to know.

"I bumped into someone's fist," he says.

"Why do boys always have to fight?" says Katie, "while girls are just so gentle and peace-loving all the time ..."

They grin at each other. Scott says, "See you later."

"You might," says Katie, "if you're very lucky."

Annette is still busy unpacking. Katie nudges me. Annette's stuff – her brushes, her creams and make-up – even her hairspray – all have labels with "A" on them. She's got food, too – not just the tea bags. The only things she hasn't labelled are her nine tins of bean salad.

"I hate her already," hisses Katie.

"If Annette hadn't come we wouldn't have been able to afford this holiday," I hiss back.

"We needed *three* people or we'd have had to cancel. Just remember that."

"I'll try," says Katie.

10.45 p.m.

Scott comes up and asks if he and Kevin can show us round tonight. Of course, we say "Yes". Scott's got dark curly hair and gypsy-boy kind of looks. He's really fit – and Katie likes him a lot. I can see why (and I'm sure he'll really go for her too).

Just down the road from our flat are masses of clubs and discos – and Scott and Kevin seem to have been to them all. They get us into this very posh place. But we don't like it much there. Everyone's looking at us. So then we go to Scott's favourite bar. It's called *Niven's* and we like it right away. It's run by three brothers from Manchester who all look exactly the same. Everyone's chatting to everyone else and having a good time.

Suddenly Katie nudges me. "That holiday feeling. It's catching!" And now I've got it too. I look around me. All this fun, all this energy and I'm part of it. Katie and I get up onto the dance floor and start singing and dancing together. People are looking at us but we don't care. We're on holiday!

A bit later on, we go to the toilets, the two of us. I say to Katie, "I think Scott really likes you."

"Can you blame him?" she grins. "And I bet Kevin fancies you."

"No, he doesn't," I say quickly. I can tell right away. Not that I'm crazy about his looks anyway. He hasn't got any lips for a start.

"Well, don't worry," says Katie. "We'll find a boy ..." she smiles, "to mend your broken heart."

"I'm so over him now," I say. I went out with this boy called ... I can't even bear to

write down his name now. But if I have to ...
Richard.

Richard dumped me, right out of the blue.
It was a big shock. And it's so boring when
you get your heart broken. You just feel
rubbish for weeks and weeks. Katie asked me
if I'd ever smile again.

But like I said, I'm so totally over him now
– and I'm really not looking for another
boyfriend.

Anyway, we're off to a foam disco now.
That should be a laugh.

More soon.

11.45 p.m.

The foam disco is brilliant. At first
everyone just stands about and looks nervous.
Then all these bubbles blow in, millions and
millions of them. They're floating
everywhere. And soon everyone's laughing
and messing about and dancing.

Katie and I start spinning round each other and dancing in our own mad way. Every time Katie shakes her blonde hair another five boys rush up. Then Katie flashes me one of her smiles, just to check I'm enjoying myself too. And I really am. Everyone is – apart from Annette.

She says the bubbles have ruined her clothes. She won't dance either. She just sits in the corner, looking very fed up. In the end, Katie bounces over to her and shouts, "Come on, Annette, let yourself go! You're on holiday," and she pulls Annette up with her and gets her to dance too.

For about five minutes Annette does join in. She even swings around and holds onto Katie's belt. But then she starts to turn green. She rushes outside where she is very sick indeed. "Katie swung me round too much," moans Annette. "Now I feel so ill." She looks terrible as well. So I have to take her back to our flat. (Katie stays behind with Scott.)

Outside the flat Annette is sick again. It slops all down the steps. The caretaker comes rushing out. He has a huge torch and he waves it at me and around the staircase. "What terrible behaviour!" he cries. "You will clean it up now." He throws a bucket and mop at the bottom of the stairs.

Annette walks upstairs slowly, holding on to the walls. I try and clean up the steps. Only I have to keep stopping because the smell is just terrible.

And then Kevin turns up with his arm round a girl I haven't seen before. He isn't expecting to see me and he shouts out, "What are you doing, Louise?"

I would have thought he could see what I was doing all too well. "Annette was sick so I'm just …"

"You can come and clean up my room too if you like," the girl butts in. Then she laughs as if she's said something hilarious.

I just look hard at her.

"Cleaning up's the caretaker's job, not yours," says Kevin. "You're on holiday. You've paid to be here."

I nod, then carry on with my work. Kevin and his girl go into his flat. Now, as I write this, I can hear Kevin and that girl giggling away together. Are they still laughing at me?

Annette is lying on her bed, groaning.

So ends my first day in Spain!

Chapter 2

The Most Annoying Girl on the Planet

Sunday 18th July

5.00 p.m.

This morning Katie, Annette and me make our first trip to the beach. We get there early – just 12 o'clock – but it's already full of wonderful golden bodies, tanned and beautiful. They're lying under huge umbrellas or walking slowly into the sea and splashing each other.

Katie gasps. "Oh, no."

"What's wrong?" I ask.

She shakes her head. She can't say anything. She's too upset to speak at first. In the end, she says, in a sad, small voice, "Everyone's so skinny." Last month Katie went for an interview to be a model. They told her to come back when she'd lost two stone. Now she goes on and on about how fat she is. I keep telling her we're not fat, we've just got big hips.

But Katie's so upset about all those thin people on the beach that she has to get something to eat. There's a whole street full of cafés and restaurants. We stop off at one. Outside there's a sign which says, "English Breakfast, just like your mum's." In fact, it's much better than anything my mum's ever cooked.

Annette says she'll pay. We can't believe it. Then she comes back from the counter with a shocked face. "When that man gave me my change he gave my hand a stroke too."

13

"This is Spain," cries Katie, "and that sort of thing happens all the time – I hope."

I call Mum just to let her know I'm still alive. She sounds so happy to hear from me, I feel a bit tearful. After the café Katie and I go back to the beach, but Annette wants to go back to the flat. She says she feels ill again.

But when we get back that evening to get ready to go out, Annette's still there. She just talks and talks.

Katie hisses at me, "Do you think if Annette keeps her mouth closed for ten seconds, her head will explode?"

1.30 a.m.

Katie and I go out with Scott and Kevin again. Annette says she'd rather stay in the flat.

As we go down the stairs, Katie says, "I could really like Scott."

"Well, what's stopping you?" I ask.

She gives a tragic smile. "The fact that he's going home tomorrow."

She goes off with Scott for a while. I sit chatting with Kevin. I ask him about the girl he was with yesterday. He just gives a shrug. Then he says, "And how's Cinderella?" That's his nickname for me after last night. He thinks it's really funny that I had to clean the stairs. He says he's going to tell his mates all about me.

When we get back to the flat the caretaker's outside. He's waiting for us. He's got that huge torch again. He stares hard at us. Katie blows him a kiss. He keeps looking at us and mutters something which sounds very rude.

"I really like you too," says Katie.

The flat is very dark. We try and creep about. But then Katie knocks something over.

It makes an awful crash. Annette jumps out of bed. "Could you please show some manners ... I was fast asleep."

"Oh, go boil your face," says Katie. Then she hisses to me, "We've gone on holiday with the most annoying girl on the planet."

Monday 19th July

4.00 p.m.

This afternoon I get stuck on the aqua-slide.

I'm half-way down and there's a bar up over my head. All I have to do is hold on to the bar and push off again. It's so simple, a child of four could do it. Only I can't. Right in the middle of the slide I just stop. And I can't push myself down any further.

IT'S A TOTAL NIGHTMARE. Everyone behind me is whistling and shouting at me to get a move on.

"I can't move, I'm stuck," I cry. In the end, I think the only thing to do is to get up and start walking down the slide. But as soon as I stand up, I slip and fall over. "Thank you so much, God," I shout. I end up whooshing down the slide on my back. I stop just before the end. Then I hit the water with a stupid little plop.

Of course, Katie and Annette are splitting their swimsuits, they're laughing so hard. So are Kevin and Scott, who came to the big pool with us.

"If your face gets any redder," calls out Katie, "the traffic will start stopping."

"I'll pay you 20 pounds if you do that again," says Scott.

"Never, never!" I cry.

Then Annette starts telling me what I did wrong. She goes on and on, all the way back to the flat.

12.45 a.m.

It's Scott and Kevin's last night. We go out with them and Annette comes too. She whispers to me that she thinks Scott is "totally buff". Doesn't she know Scott is mad about Katie?

She keeps smiling at Scott. He just looks puzzled. A bit later, Annette sees that Scott's all over Katie and she storms off.

When Kevin and Scott say "Goodbye" I feel really sad. We've only known them for two days but they feel like real friends. We swap addresses. As soon as they've gone Katie says, "I'll only keep their addresses for a few days. I'll have forgotten who they are by next week."

Even so, she looks dead upset.

Tuesday 20th July

Katie – who can be a bit naughty – has started moving Annette's pots and creams about. Of course Annette's really mad at her.

Katie and I spend the whole day on the beach. We find the fattest people we can and lie next to them.

Wednesday 21st July

7.00 a.m!!

We got woken up at half past six in the morning by Annette. She's screaming blue murder. Katie and I jump out of bed. Annette says there's an animal in the bathroom.

"I could feel it on the mat … and it touched me," she yells.

Katie and I creep into the bathroom. We peer down at the mat and see … three hairs.

Katie says to me, "Before this holiday is over I think I may kill Annette."

8.00 p.m.

This evening Katie and I put all our clothes out on the bed as we just can't decide what to wear.

"You two," says Annette, shaking her head. "You're so funny."

"She thinks we're funny," Katie says out loud.

"Oh, well," I say. "You've got to admit, she's got personality."

"Yeah and all of it bad," replies Katie.

Chapter 3

Hearing a Secret

Thursday 22ⁿᵈ July

Annette spends the day by the pool on her own. And she says she's too tired to come out with us this evening.

"Do you think she's OK?"

"Oh, yes," says Katie. "If she wants to act as if she's 150 ... let her. And I bet she'll have a lovely time checking no-one's touched her hand cream, or her lovely bean salads."

Katie and I go to *Niven's* first. We know quite a few people there now and they're all a good laugh. The three brothers who run it tell lots of jokes, and the music's brilliant. They call Katie and me the *London Girls*.

Next we go to a disco. Katie and I are pretty good at blanking out boys we don't like. Katie's not keen on anyone wearing Union Jack shorts – or who's got loads of tattoos. But she still ends up doing a slow dance with this lad she calls "Mr Tonsils" because he keeps trying to stick his tongue down her throat!

I've got stuck with this boy who dances so close, I have to peel him off me when the music stops.

Then this tall, blonde guy turns up. He's good-looking but looks as if he knows it. I say, "I bet he spends most of his life in front of the mirror."

Katie doesn't answer. But I see her looking at him. He spots Katie too. Then he suddenly rushes over, grabs Katie and says,

"Excuse me. I've got to talk to this girl. We're in love."

I look at him. I don't trust him. But Katie dashes off with him. She comes back later. She's all smiles. She says, "He's interesting, and a bit different. He's called Andrew."

Andrew brings over his mate, Lee, to meet me.

"There you go," hisses Katie.

Lee's quite good fun. But he doesn't fancy me. Like I told you, I can always tell.

Katie wants Andrew and Lee to come back to our flat. I remind her that Annette's there and that, most likely, she'll be asleep. "We're on holiday, not at boarding school," Katie snaps.

But, in the end, we agree to meet Andrew and Lee on the beach tomorrow. Then Katie and I go back to our flat. It's very dark and very hot. Annette's shut all the windows, to stop the mosquitoes getting in.

"This is awful," says Katie. "It's much too dark and depressing." She flings open all the windows.

Then we sit together and talk in whispers for hours.

"I still miss Scott," Katie says. "But I do like Andrew as well."

"I think the only person Andrew loves is himself," I say.

"All boys love themselves," replies Katie. "Andrew's just more open about it." Then she starts talking about me and my love life.

"Are you sure Lee doesn't fancy you?"

I nod. I'm sure.

"But you're so pretty," Katie goes on, "boys should be flocking round you. Perhaps you're giving off the wrong signals. It's because you're still thinking about Richard."

"No, I'm not," I say at once.

"Don't let him get in the way and spoil this holiday," says Katie.

I stare at her. "He really isn't. I'm totally over him. And I don't need a boyfriend to have a good time. I promise."

I'm not sure Katie believes me.

Friday 23rd July

This afternoon Andrew takes Katie off to have a swim in the pool. I'm sitting on the beach on my own when this girl plonks down beside me.

I met her at *Niven's*. She's quite pretty with long blonde hair and her name is Becky. She chats to me as if we're old friends. This is rather puzzling.

Then she asks if Katie's with Andrew.
I say she is. A funny look comes into Becky's
eyes. "I heard Andrew on the phone last
night. He was talking away to this girl for
ages saying how he loved her and missed her.
I just thought you should know about it ..."

Why tell me? Is Becky jealous of Katie?
Or is she just a bit spiteful?

What should I do?

I make up my mind I won't tell Katie.
She's only having a bit of fun with Andrew.
Why should I spoil it?

Chapter 4

Annette Leaves

Saturday 24th July

Something amazing happens tonight – Annette gets chatted up. Her nose turns bright red with excitement.

Her fan isn't very good-looking. In fact, he's short and nearly bald. And when he smiles his eyes pop right out of his head. Katie thinks there's something spooky about him.

"Oh, no," I reply. "He's just a nice, harmless idiot."

Then Annette tells us she's taking him back to our flat. Now that does make me nervous. After a bit Katie and I go back to the flat too. Andrew comes with us. Andrew's friend, Lee, has spent the evening with his arm around another girl. But do I care? I really do not.

Outside our flat, Andrew says, "We'd better make a noise ... just in case."

That makes Katie get the giggles. "Stop laughing," whispers Andrew. That only makes Katie laugh more.

We open the door. It's very dark and very quiet.

"We know what you're doing," calls out Andrew. "Come on, get your clothes back on."

Two faces peep round the balcony.

Annette's boyfriend gives us one of his mad smiles. He says, "It's OK, we knew you were there."

But Annette is mad with us. "How dare you shout out things like that. I'm not that sort of girl – unlike you two."

We let that go. Then Annette shouts, "You've spoilt everything tonight ..."

"Oh, we're sorry," cries Katie. "We were just having a bit of fun with you."

But Annette's very angry indeed. She says, "Come on, Vernon, let's go."

And they march out together.

"He's called Vernon," shouts Katie and we all fall about laughing. We're still laughing when Annette rushes back – on her own.

"Where's the lovely Vernon gone?" asks Katie.

Annette's out of breath. She can't say anything to begin with. In the end she gasps out, "Vernon's just been attacked."

We're all listening then.

"Who's attacked him?" asks Andrew.

"The caretaker," Annette sobs. "We were waiting for the lift and it was taking ages. So Vernon gave it a very soft tap. And then the caretaker just turned up on the stairs, from nowhere ..." Her voice begins to shake. "He said Vernon was a vandal. Then he started hitting Vernon over the head with that huge torch he carries ..."

"Oh no," splutters Katie. She's trying so hard not to laugh. "What did Vernon do then?"

"What could he do?" cries Annette. "He ran off. He never even said "Good night" to me."

"That's terrible," I say.

"I wish I'd seen it," hisses Katie.

"This is all just a joke to you, isn't it?" snaps Annette.

"No, it isn't. I'm really sorry," says Katie. She sounds as if she means it this time and Annette stops and looks at her. But then Katie spoils everything by laughing like crazy. "I'm sorry," she splutters, "it's just thinking of Vernon running for his life."

"Oh, shut up," says Annette. Then she goes into a sulk and won't talk to any of us.

5.00 a.m.

NEWS FLASH

I've been woken up by the sound of someone moving about in our room. I think we've got burglars. I climb out of bed but I'm feeling very scared. What should I do? My heart's thumping like crazy. I feel sick with fear. Then I see Annette ... packing.

"What are you doing?" I cry.

"Getting the next plane out of here," she says.

"But why?" I whisper.

"Because I hate it here. All you and Katie do is laugh and make fun of me."

"No, we don't ... look, I'm sorry if we've upset you. But we didn't mean to. And we do like you," I add.

"No, you don't," says Annette.

I spend the next 30 minutes telling Annette how much we like her. And that she mustn't think of going home now.

I think Katie's fast asleep all this time. But when I say to Annette, "This holiday just won't be the same without you ..." Katie says softly, "No, it'll be better."

In the end, Annette agrees to stay until the morning. We're just settling down to sleep again when Katie murmurs, "Do you think Vernon's stopped running yet?"

Then she gives her loudest laugh yet. Annette says firmly, "That's it. No way am I staying on here. Louise is OK but you just don't know when to stop!"

Sunday 25th July

10.00 a.m.

When I wake up Annette's gone. She's taken all her stuff too. Katie's still fast asleep. So I set off to find Annette on my own. I find her quite easily. She's sitting outside the café where we had breakfast the other day. I think she's been crying. I sit down beside her.

"I don't want to stay here," she says, "but I don't want to go home either."

She then tells me how she hates it at home because her mum's just got a new boyfriend. She and the new boyfriend are always on the couch. They hold hands and giggle ...

"Oh, that's so gross," I say.

"I have to live in my bedroom now," she says. "That's why I wanted to come on this holiday so much ... but it's all gone wrong."

"No, it hasn't," I say.

"Do you think Vernon will come and find me today?" she asks.

"I'm sure he will," I say. I really do try and cheer her up. Then Annette tells me how much she admires Katie. I can't believe what I'm hearing.

"I know she can be rude," she says, "but she's so funny, isn't she?"

I nod my head.

"And everyone likes her, don't they?
I expect that's why you follow her around all the time."

"I don't follow her around at all," I snap back. I think I've spent enough time now trying to cheer Annette up.

11.00 a.m.

I get back to the flat to find a note from Katie. She says she's gone off with Andrew for the day and won't be back until tonight. I feel a bit hurt about the way Katie has just run off. She never even asked if I wanted to go along. Then, all at once, I think about what Annette said. About how I always tag along behind Katie. It really isn't true. It's just she's less shy than me. So I like her to get things going. That's all.

11.30 a.m.

I DO NOT FOLLOW KATIE AROUND. Yes, I'm still thinking about that. I don't want to – but I can't help it.

11.30 p.m.

Katie's not back yet. And Annette's upset again. Vernon hasn't been to see her.

I'm having an early night. Right now, to be honest, I feel a bit low. I'm not sure why.

It isn't because I haven't met a boy I like (or who likes me). It really isn't.

But, even so, I do feel a tiny bit jealous of Katie and Andrew. Andrew's not my type at all.

Somewhere in Spain there must be one boy who fancies me a little bit.

Chapter 5
Saving Mark

Monday 26th July

Katie's gone off with Andrew again. He's taking her out in a boat. "I like him more and more," says Katie, softly, as if she can't believe what's happening. Maybe I should say something about this other girl he was ringing? I don't think I will. Why spoil Katie's day?

I spend the afternoon on the beach with Annette. She lies there talking, talking, talking ... then some boys come by and pretend to chat us up. Their club needs some new people and they've been sent out to find some. They're just trying to get us to go there tonight.

But Annette is taken in. She's so excited I don't want to tell her the truth. I even agree to go to the club with her.

7.00 p.m.

Annette's been shopping and she's got some new clothes – these trousers which are very tight. Not a good idea on someone who's got a big bum. Bitchy, but true. She thinks she looks great. "Hey, Louise, let's go clubbing," she calls out.

Annette – the party animal. Can you believe it?

9.00 p.m.

The club isn't bad. "Look at all those fancy mirrors," cries Annette. She thinks it's really quite posh.

But the drinks cost way too much. What a total rip-off!

A wet T-shirt competition starts up. And, there, watching, is ... Vernon. Annette sees him and gives him a big friendly wave. Vernon gives a much less friendly wave back. And then he just vanishes. Annette can't believe it.

"Why didn't he stay?" she says. "He never even said hello to me."

"Boys are like that," I mutter. I see Vernon again a bit later. He's with a small, red-haired girl. I don't tell Annette.

I want to go on to *Niven's* now. But Annette's having too much fun with a Spanish guy who can't speak one word of English. I'll have to stay here a bit longer.

2.30 a.m.

What a night! So much has happened.

I'm still in the posh club with Annette when I see a boy looking at me. He's not very good-looking but I like his face. It's interesting. The kind of face you want to look at twice. So I do just that.

And then he walks across to talk to me. He's tall and has a lovely, friendly smile. "Hi, I'm Mark. What's your name?" he says.

I smile back at him. "I'm Louise."

Then we go through that awful bit where you say stuff about yourself. He tells me he's been to Spain before but not this part. He only arrived here this afternoon. Then he asks me if I want a drink. We go up to the bar and he buys me a very fizzy drink, which he says comes from this part of Spain.

"It's quite strong," he says. "So you'd better hold your nose before you drink it."

One sip is plenty. I don't want any more. *This is what petrol must taste like*, I think to myself. Mark downs his drink in one.

"Lovely stuff," he says, and he smacks his lips.

Two seconds later he's fallen on to a table.

At first I think he's messing about. But then he gasps, "It doesn't normally get me like this. I haven't eaten all day." He staggers to his feet.

"Can I do anything?" I ask.

He smiles at me. "Thanks, but I'll be OK. I won't be long so don't move." Then he stumbles to the door. *Should I go after him?* I ask myself. He doesn't look at all well.

After a few minutes I get up and look around outside. I can't see him anywhere. Maybe he's gone home. He said his flat's near here. I'm surprised at how let-down I feel.

I go back into the disco. Then I spot Mark in the doorway ... He's swaying about, and he's covered in blood. He looks like someone out of a horror movie. I can see he's in pain.

But the doormen won't let him in. I rush over.

"Mark, what happened?" I say.

"I just went outside and this gang of guys jumped me," he says.

"Oh no."

"They took all my money as well. I'm quite a good fighter – but there were five of them. I had no chance."

"Poor Mark," I murmur. "You need to put some cold water on your cuts. Just lean on me," and I walk him round the outside of the club to the toilets.

Mark's so dazed he doesn't see I'm taking him into the Ladies.

He sits down on the floor while I clean him up. He starts to sniff so I say, "Don't cry, Mark. You'll be OK."

"I'm not crying," he replies. "I'm just in shock."

When we come out of the Ladies, Annette spots Mark and me together, with our arms round each other. She'd come outside to see where I was. "Louise, what's going on?" she asks. When I tell her what's happened she wants to help.

We stagger up the road with Mark between us. Even with two of us helping him along, he's very heavy. "Are we anywhere near your place yet?" I ask. Both Annette and I are panting.

Mark looks around. "I think we're going in the wrong direction," he manages to say.

A little later Mark admits he's totally forgotten where he lives. So Annette and I agree that, just for tonight, he can crash out in our flat.

By the time Katie comes back Mark is fast asleep on my sofa-bed.

"And where did *he* come from?" Katie wants to know.

"Louise picked him up," says Annette. "She was in the Ladies with him for ages."

"Thanks so much for that, Annette," I say. I have to tell Katie everything that's happened.

"Do you believe his story?" Katie asks.

"What do you mean?"

"Well, he might be a terrorist on the run or ..."

"Oh no, he's not," I say. "I know he's not." Katie grins at me. Just then, Mark opens his eyes and tries to sit up. He looks dazed.

"It's OK," I say. "You're in our flat."

He stares at me for a moment then says, "Louise."

"That's right."

He repeats my name and goes back to sleep again.

"Boys always look so sweet when they're asleep, don't they?" says Katie.

"Yes, they do," I agree. Katie starts laughing. I must have sounded too keen.

Now I'm writing this in Katie's bed. Katie's snoring softly. In fact, everyone's been asleep for ages except for me. I don't think I'll get to sleep for a long time. I'm squashed and hot and – very happy.

Chapter 6
Under the Bed

Tuesday 27th July

Mark says that when he woke up this morning he hadn't a clue where he was. Then he saw all these cute(!) girls walking about in bikinis and he thought he must be in heaven. When we hear that, we want Mark to stay for toast and coffee.

Then Katie spots this guy with his girlfriend on the balcony below ours. They're lying together, sunbathing. "Aaah, how romantic," she says. Then she gets her towel, puts it under the tap and squeezes out the water on them.

They both jump into the air as if they've been stung. Then they run inside.

"Excellent," Katie shouts. "I think there's going to be a water fight."

Katie, Mark and myself go and fill up some water bottles and rush out on to the balcony. Annette joins us too!

We're all ready for a good water fight when there's a knock on the door. Someone says in a very cross voice, "Open up, this is the caretaker."

We all just freeze.

Then the caretaker shouts out, "Open up! I have had complaints about you of a serious nature ..."

Katie whispers, "I bet those people downstairs told him about those tiny drops of water I threw on them. How boring are they! Well, we won't answer the door. Don't anyone make a noise."

In fact, Katie has been doing all the talking. Even so, we keep very quiet for a few minutes.

"He must have gone by now," whispers Katie.

But then Annette shouts, "Listen."

We can hear the caretaker knocking on the door of the flat next to us. Then we hear him talking to them. The next thing we hear is his voice on *their* balcony. He must be trying to climb over their balcony and on to ours.

"You'd better hide under the bed, Mark," hisses Annette.

We all stare at her. "Well, look how the caretaker attacked Vernon," she shouts.

"That's true," I say. "And you've already been beaten up once, Mark."

Mark slides under the bed. He says, "If you need any help ..."

"We'll pull you out at once," says Katie. Then she says to Annette, "This is all my fault, isn't it?"

I wait for Annette to agree. But she just mutters, "You only wanted to have some fun, Katie." I can't believe it.

The three of us go out on to the balcony just as the caretaker is climbing over. He's purple with rage.

"Why didn't you come to your door when I knocked?" he roars.

"Didn't hear you. Sorry," says Katie. But even she shakes as she says it.

The caretaker turns on Annette. "Have you been throwing water about?" he asks.

He's still got his torch even though it's the morning. He waves it at her face.

"Maybe," says Annette. I can't get over how brave she's being.

"It was all of us," I say. We link hands and the caretaker glares at us all. Then he starts moaning on and on about how he knew we were trouble. And if anybody else complains about us he'll throw us out on to the street.

"I can do that, you know," he says. "And I promise you, I will." Then he marches off.

"Phew," says Katie.

"Well done," says Mark. He pops out from under the bed. Just then there's another knock on the door.

"It's him again!" shouts Katie. She pushes Mark back under the bed.

But this time it's two of Mark's friends. They've been looking for him because he didn't come back last night. Somehow, they found out he was here.

"Is Mark about?" they ask.

"Oh, yes," says Katie. She's grinning like crazy now. "You'll find him under our bed."

We all have lunch together. Then Mark goes off with his mates. He needs to get some more money. I offer to lend him some but he won't hear of it. Mark says he wants to see me again – tonight!!

Wednesday 28th July

2.00 p.m.

Just seen Mark. He says he and his friends are going to try and find that gang who attacked him. He's even renting a jeep for the day.

"Oh, please – no. No more fights," I beg.

Mark shakes his head sadly. "Sorry Louise, but I can't promise that."

3.00 p.m.

Lying on the beach with Katie, I can't stop thinking about Mark. I'm scared. I don't want him to get into another fight.

"Oh, stop looking as if your husband's just gone off to war ..." Katie says. "Boys are all mouth. I bet he won't really *do* anything." Then she adds, "I'm glad you've found Mark. But don't get too carried away. This is just for laughs – OK?"

"How about you and Andrew?" I ask.

"We're just having a good time. It's nothing serious," she replies.

But I don't believe her. I think she's mad about Andrew.

6.00 p.m.

Still no sign of Mark.

9.00 p.m.

Mark's back! He says they found the gang in a bar. But when the gang spotted Mark they ran off out of the bar by the back door. "What a bunch of cowards!" Mark says.

Katie looks at Mark. "I don't believe a word," she mutters softly to me.

I'm just glad Mark is safe.

Anyway, here's the big news – Mark's asked me out for a meal tomorrow – just the two of us. What did I say? Yes, Yes, Yes, Yes!

Only I didn't say, "Yes" four times. I was a bit more cool about it. But that's what I was saying in my head.

Thursday 29th July

1.30 a.m.

My meal with Mark.

Mark takes me to this really posh place. I'm not sure he can afford it, after all, he's had some of his money stolen. But he says it's fine.

For the first time I don't choose food from the tourist menu. No, this time I think I'll be a bit brave. So I have *Tortilla Espanola*. That's a thick omelette with potatoes and onions inside it. But I don't really notice what I'm eating.

Mark keeps asking me if I'm having a good time. And whenever I say anything funny, he just explodes laughing. I think he's a bit nervous – and that makes me like him even more. He really wants tonight to go well.

Mark talks about his family (he's got three brothers) and his job (he works in an electrical shop). I listen hard. It might not sound very interesting – but it is to me. I start making up pictures in my mind about what his life is like. Then I begin to think about meeting Marks' parents and brothers.

I start to think about what it would be like to go out with Mark back home. I know it's silly but I can't stop.

It's late when I get back to the flat. Katie and Annette are waiting for me. They want to know about everything that's happened.

"If only he lived down the road and not in Glasgow," I say. "If only tomorrow wasn't our last full day."

Katie squeezes my hand. "Sometimes," she says, "life sucks."

2.30 a.m.

I can't tell anyone – not even Katie – how much I like Mark. It's so stupid, isn't it? I've only known him for three days. And when I leave on Saturday I'll probably never see him again.

I know all that. And I'm still mad about him.

Chapter 7

The Night We Didn't Sleep

Friday 30ᵗʰ July

10.00 a.m.

"We've nothing to go back for, have we?" says Katie. We start the day talking about how we can stay in Spain. "If you will, I will," we say to each other. But really we know it's no good. We've got no money for a start. We can't just stay on now. We need a proper plan.

I know we have to go home tomorrow. But I really hate to leave everyone ... most of all you know who.

In the afternoon we start our goodbyes by walking round the whole town. We take thousands of pictures. We want to remember everything. Annette comes with us. She says, "I don't want to go back. I like it here now."

I never thought Annette would ever fit in. Yet, she does now. Well, sort of anyway. This afternoon a boy rushes up to Annette and says, "Someone told me to give this to you." He puts a beautiful red rose in her hand, and then legs it.

Annette hasn't a clue who the rose could be from.

And neither have we!

"Maybe it's a joke," Katie whispers.

Annette is so happy. She murmurs over and over again, "I've got a secret admirer."

We meet up with Mark and Andrew. We all play mini-golf and have a great meal together. Afterwards we snap still more pictures. Andrew is very witty and fun. I can see why Katie likes him. But, like I said, he's not my type.

Andrew's just a big show-off. Mark's so much more than that.

Then we do our last tour of the nightclubs and bars. As soon as we walk into *Niven's*, Jim, one of the brothers from Manchester yells, "And this song is dedicated to the London Girls, who've got to go home tomorrow." Everyone goes "Aaah". "Come back any time you want, girls!"

The song he puts on is an old one, but Katie and I really like it. *Girls just wanna have fun.* You can hardly hear it because there's so much clapping and cheering.

"You've made a lot of friends here," says Jim.

After that, everyone comes up to give us hugs and cuddles. They tell us how much they're going to miss us. In the end I have to walk away or I'll start crying my eyes out. It's funny, I've only known these people a short time. Yet, right now, I feel closer to them than most of my friends at school.

At the disco later, Katie comes over and says, "Guess what? Mark's just told me he loves you." That makes me feel so happy and so sad at the same time. It's odd.

Katie and I think tonight is too special for sleeping. Instead, we're going to sit on the beach and wait for the sunrise.

5.30 a.m.

A perfect night, and I've never felt more wide-awake.

Andrew, Katie, Mark and myself all lie on the beach. Annette's there too. I hope she doesn't feel left out – she's the only one without a boyfriend. But she seems really happy tonight. She sits there, with the red rose in her hair, and she says bits of poems out loud. It all adds to the feeling. It doesn't matter that all the poems she knows are about people dying in World War I.

Then Andrew asks Katie to go for a walk with him. They're gone for ages. When they come back Katie whispers to me what happened. Andrew told her he has a girlfriend at home. It's the first Katie knows about it. Now Andrew wants to dump the old girlfriend and go out with Katie instead.

"So what are you going to do?" I ask.

"I don't know," she murmurs. "Keep your voice down. I don't want Annette to hear all this." Then she gives a huge sigh. "How can I make my mind up about anything? Nothing's real here, is it?"

I nod. But I'm thinking about Mark. When he said he loved me – was that real? The question races round and round in my head.

Then the sky starts to turn a wonderful pink-orange colour. Katie and Andrew dive into the sea for a last mad swim, while Mark and I just lie there together, watching all the colours of the morning slowly returning. This has got to be the most romantic moment of my entire life. In fact, I suppose it's the only romantic one.

Right now, everything is just perfect. Home seems further away than the moon.

Saturday 31st July

We lie on the beach until the very last moment. Then we fling everything into our cases. (Katie never took much of her stuff out.) The caretaker stands outside his office. He's still got his torch. He holds it as if it's a sword.

"I just want to say," Katie tells him, "that I think you're very sexy. I love the way you always leave some of your breakfast in your beard. That makes you look so hot."

"You go off and don't come back!" he snarls.

Katie calls out, "Missing you already!" She blows him a big kiss. Then the three of us run back to the beach. Mark and Andrew are still there, but fast asleep.

"Aaah, look at them," says Katie.

We wake them up. Then we all rush into the town centre. The coach is about to go.

"Did Katie tell you what I said?" mumbles Mark.

"Yes," I reply.

"Well, I mean it."

The driver bangs on the window. We need to go!

"I'll text you every day," says Mark. "And I'll come to see you very soon."

It takes a long time but in the end Katie and I get slowly on to the coach. Annette has saved a seat for us, right at the back.

Katie gives my hand a squeeze. "It'll be OK," she says. She's in more of a state than me. Our faces are glued to the window and we wave and wave until we can't see Andrew and Mark any more. They've taken our holiday with them.

There's nothing left but the long journey back home.

"This has been the best holiday ever," I say.

Katie doesn't say anything. Instead, she starts singing, "We're off to sunny Spain." Some of the other people in the coach turn round to look at her. They don't know who's being so stupid and loud. Annette and I join in. Soon we start clapping our hands and tapping our feet too. It's like that first night when we started singing together. But this time the tears fall down our faces.

Katie doesn't say a word about Andrew. But I saw her put his address carefully in her bag. As for me – well, right now, I think I'm in love with Mark.

Maybe in a few months time I'll look at what I've written – and shake my head and smile. Perhaps by then Mark will just be a holiday romance I once had.

But, maybe ... maybe Mark will be my true love forever.

I just don't know.

I can only hope.

Adios for now.

Barrington Stoke would like to thank all its readers for commenting on the manuscript before publication and in particular:

Stephanie Arnold
Charlotte Barnett
Chelsea Bayley
William Blanchard
Victoria Belton
Charlotte Bence
Josie Bond
Katy Burke
Natalie Cadman
Brittany Coates
Laura Gribble
Kerry-Marie Grundy
Stephanie Gunning
Bekie Jones
Anthony Lawrence
Jade Lenthall

Mrs Alwyn Martin
Joseph Martin
Emma McNicholas
Stephanie Mullin
Daniel Pearce
Shauny Price
Jenni Rawlings
Natalie Stephens
Anna Strand
Danielle Teal
Mrs Tina van Tricht
Marie Ann Welsh
Katie Wilcox
Becky Wilson
Mrs Jacqueline Wilson
Claire Winship

Become a Consultant!

Would you like to give us feedback on our titles before they are published? Contact us at the email address below – we'd love to hear from you!

info@barringtonstoke.co.uk
www.barringtonstoke.co.uk

If you loved this book, why don't you read ...

Diary of an (Un)teenager

by Pete Johnson

ISBN 1-842991-51-5

Sunday 21st June

"... I won't have anything to do with designer clothes, or girls, or body piercing, or any of it ... no, I shall let it all pass me by. Do you know what I'm going to be? An (Un)teenager.

But then Spencer's best mate Zac starts wearing baggy trousers and huge trainers – and even starts going on dates with girls. But Spencer is determined: "Dear diary, I am going to stay EXACTLY as I am now. That's a promise ..."

A hilarious comedy by the "devastatingly funny Pete Johnson". *Sunday Times*

You can order **Diary of an (Un)teenager** directly from our website at **www.barringtonstoke.co.uk**